To Alan - not least for the nose -
and to Scott and Holly

First published in Great Britain in 1993 by
Simon & Schuster Young Books
Campus 400
Maylands Avenue
Hemel Hempstead HP2 7EZ

Typeset in 18/25pt Bookman by Goodfellow & Egan Ltd, Cambridge
Printed and bound in Belgium by Proost International Book Productions

British Library Cataloguing in Publication Data available

ISBN 0-7500-1250-1
ISBN 0-7500-1251-X

Baby Bear's Nose

Penny McKinlay

Illustrated by Siobhan Dodds

SIMON & SCHUSTER
YOUNG BOOKS

Baby Bear was bouncing on Mummy Bear's knee. She was tickling him and cuddling him and kissing him on the nose.

Suddenly Mummy Bear turned to Daddy Bear.
"I think he's getting your nose, dear," she said.

Baby Bear's nose was
a shiny little black button
that sat in the middle of his face.
Daddy Bear's nose was a great
long furry black snout, and
Baby Bear couldn't see how it
would fit on his face at all.

He got down from Mummy Bear's knee
and looked at himself in the mirror.
"I shall just have to go and find a nose for
myself," he said sadly.
And off he went.

First Baby Bear saw a duck
swimming in the pond.

"Hello, Duck," said Baby Bear.
"Could I try on your nose, please?"
"It's not a nose, it's a *beak*," quacked
the duck, as he handed it over.

Baby Bear didn't like the beak at all.
It was bright yellow and very damp
with bits of weed hanging from it.
"And it will be very hard to nuzzle
into Mummy's neck at bedtime,"
thought Baby Bear.

There was a pigsty near Duck's pond. Fat Pig had his head stuck in a bucket of pig swill.

"Excuse me, Pig," said Baby Bear.
"Could I try on your nose, please?"
"It's not a nose, it's a *snout*," grunted Pig, as he handed it over.

But Pig's snout didn't look at all right. It was
pink and wobbly, and it wasn't very clean.
"Pig doesn't take very good care of his nose,"
thought Baby Bear. "It's still got some
dinner stuck to it."

Further on, Baby Bear nearly bumped
into a rhinoceros.

"Please could I try on your nose,
Rhinoceros," said Baby Bear, standing
well clear of the horn.
"Of course," snorted the Rhinoceros, "but be
careful, this horn is very sharp, you know."

But the horn on
Rhinoceros's nose was so
big and heavy that Baby Bear could hardly
lift his head.
"Phew!" he gasped. "I wouldn't get very far
with a nose like that."

Round the corner, Baby Bear came
face-to-face with an elephant!

"Please, Mr Elephant,
could I try on your nose?"
asked Baby Bear politely.

"It's not a nose, it's a *trunk*,"
harumphed the elephant crossly.
And he handed it over.

But the Elephant's trunk looked
quite wrong on Baby Bear's face.
It was all grey and wrinkled and
Baby Bear kept tripping over it.

"This nose seems to have a mind of its own," thought Baby Bear nervously.

Baby Bear ran on, and suddenly he found himself nose-to-nose with a crocodile!

"P-p-p-please, Mr Crocodile," stammered Baby Bear. "Could I try your nose on?"

"Certainly," grinned the Crocodile,
and handed it over.

"Ooooh...er!" gasped Baby Bear, as he caught sight of his reflection in the water. It was green and scaly, bristling with sharp teeth.

"That nose would frighten me every time
I saw it," thought Baby Bear. "And it
would never fit inside a honey pot."

Baby Bear was feeling a bit shakey and very
tired, and he decided to go home for tea.

It was a special tea of cakes and honey, and
soon Baby Bear quite forgot about his nose.

Until one day, many years later, when he
was no longer a Baby Bear but actually quite
a Big Bear with baby bears of his own.
He looked in the mirror, and there he saw
his Daddy's nose.

And it looked just right.